THE GALAXY'S GREATEST COMIC...

Published in the UK on 26 February 1977, Prog 1 of *2000 AD* ushered in a new era of sci-fi action and adventure for comic readers, dazzling them with a mind-blowing array of fantastic futures and shocking possibilities. Appearing for the first time in Prog 2, *Judge Dredd* made a huge and instant impression with readers and remains the mainstay of *2000 AD* to this day. In the twenty-four years and 1250 (and counting) progs that followed, *2000 AD* has continued to thrill and inspire legions of fans, with memorable strips such as *A.B.C Warriors*, *D.R. & Quinch*, *The Ballad of Halo Jones*, *Nemesis the Warlock*, *Robo-Hunter*, *Strontium Dog* and *Zenith* (to mention but a few).

2000 AD was the proving ground for a host of A-list British writers and artists, now recognised both sides of the Atlantic. Luminaries to emerge from under the wing of Tharg The Mighty (*2000 AD*'s alien editor for the uninitiated) include Brian Bolland, Garth Ennis, Alan Grant, Alan Moore, Grant Morrison, Frank Quitely and many, many more.

Titan Books' links with *2000 AD* go back almost to the very beginning, with the publication of the first graphic novel collection, *The Chronicles of Judge Dredd*, back in July 1981.

Mega-Speak

2000 AD introduced fans not only to new worlds and new characters, but also to a whole new language. From the alien utterings of Tharg ("Zarjaz", which means great, "Thrill-power", which quantified the amount of excitement in a given strip, and "Borag Thungg", a greeting, became common parlance among fans of the comic) to the street lingo of Mega-City One, *2000 AD* quickly developed its very own dictionary. For those unfamiliar with the world of Judge Dredd, here's a handy guide to Mega-speak:

PSI-JUDGE

ROOKIE

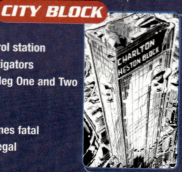

CITY BLOCK

BLOCK WAR: Conflict between rival City Blocks
BIRDIE: Lie-detector
BLITZER: Assassin
BODY-SHARKING: Illegal dealing in the bodies of living humans
BOING!: Miracle rubber
CITY BLOCK: Towering developments, housing over 50,000 citizens
DROKK: Local exclamation!
FATTIES: Obese citizens
FUTSIE: Person suffering from future-shock
GILA-MUNJA: Cursed Earth mutants used as assassins
GRUD: God
HONDO CITY: Japan
H-WAGON: Justice Department flying transport
I-BLOCK: Justice Department safe-house
ISO-CUBE: Individual cells, housed in high security prisons
JIMP: Judge impersonator
JUVES: Youngsters
JUVE CUBE: Similar to Iso-Cubes, for young offenders
LAWGIVER: Judge's multi-faceted gun
LAWMASTER: Judge's high-powered motorbike

LONG WALK: Judge retirement in the Cursed Earth
MO-PAD: Mobile home
MUTIE: Cursed Earth mutant
OZ: Australia
PERP: Perpetrator, criminal
PERP-RUNNING: Illegal transportation of wanted criminals
PLASTEEN: All-purpose building material
PSI-JUDGE: Judge with telepathic abilities
RADLANDS: Radioactive wasteland
RESYK: Human corpse recycling plant
ROOKIE: Judge in training
SCRAWLER: Graffiti artist
SECTOR HOUSE: Justice Department control station
SJS: Special Judicial Squad; Judge investigators
SOV-BLOCK: Formerly Russia, now East-Meg One and Two
STOOKIE-GLAND: Anti-aging drug. Illegal
STUB GUN: Hand-held laser rifle
STUMM GAS: Last-resort riot gas, sometimes fatal
UMPTY CANDY: Highly addictive sweet. Illegal
WALLY SQUAD: Undercover Judges

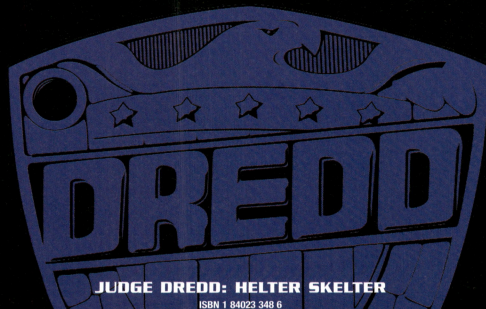

JUDGE DREDD: HELTER SKELTER

ISBN 1 84023 348 6

Published by Titan Books, a division of Titan Publishing Group Ltd.
144 Southwark St
London SE1 0UP
In association with Rebellion

A CIP catalogue record for this title is available from the British Library.

First edition: February 2002
1 3 5 7 9 10 8 6 4 2

Cover illustration by Glenn Fabry.

Printed in Italy.
Other *2000 AD* titles now available from Titan Books:

Judge Dredd: Emerald Isle (ISBN: 1 84023 341 9)
Judge Dredd: Death Aid (ISBN: 1 84023 344 3)
Judge Dredd featuring Judge Death (ISBN: 1 84023 386 9)
Judge Dredd : Goodnight Kiss (ISBN: 1 84023 346 X)

The Complete Ballad of Halo Jones (ISBN: 1 84023 342 7)
Zenith: Phase One (ISBN: 1 84023 343 5)
The Complete D.R. & Quinch (ISBN: 1 84023 345 1)

To order telephone 01536 764 646 ext. 21

What did you think of this book? We love to hear from our readers. Please email us at: readerfeedback@titanemail.com, or write to us at the above address.

Rogues' Gallery

'Helter Skelter' features the return of some of Dredd's most fearsome (and dead!) enemies. For those not versed in over 20 years of *Dredd* continuity, here's a handy guide to the scum of Mega-City One...

Chief Judge Cal

First appearance: Prog #86
Beginning his career in the elite SJS – the Judges' Internal Affairs unit – nobody realised that Cal was insane until it was far too late: he was Chief Judge by that stage! He died when Fergee, an ally of Dredd from the Undercity, hurled himself (and Cal) from the top of the Statue of Judgement and saved Mega-City One from a planned gas attack.

War Marshal Kazan

First appearance: Prog #250
Leader of the East-Meg One strike which began the Apocalypse War – a vast conflict that saw much of Mega-City One destroyed – "Mad Dog" Kazan was the Sov-Bloc's most feared Judge, assassinating his own Direktorat and declaring himself East-Meg's new Chief Judge – a position that lasted until Dredd executed him for war crimes…

Don Uggie Apelino

First appearance: Prog #39
Don Apelino fell foul of Dredd several times – during a gang war, and later after an attempt to have Dredd assassinated – before the radiation fallout from the Apocalypse War regressed him to the intelligence of a normal ape, whereupon he led a group of murderous apes in the Cursed Earth – and ran into Dredd for the last time.

Grampus

First appearance: Prog #94
Klegg mercenary Grampus was appointed Deputy Chief Judge by Cal, following the help he gave Cal in taking over Mega-City One. Responsible for ludicrously harsh laws and an attempt to kill Dredd and the anti-Cal rebels, Grampus was killed during the final battle to retake the City.

Fink Angel

First appearance: Prog #193
Fink lived in a hole from the age of seven, and chose the Cursed Earth as his home. Its radiation changed him into a terrifying mutant, and when he heard that Dredd had wiped out his family, he and his mutant rat companion tried several times to get revenge. Fink finally fell victim to his own trap –the "Pa Angel Mark One Super-Scream Torture Machine"!

Captain Skank

First appearance: Prog #197
Metal-haired mutant Captain Skank was a pirate in the Black Atlantic, until he kidnapped a Mega-City scientist and launched the nuclear weapons on his floating fortress, wiping out an entire City Block and murdering around 4,000,000 people. The Judges boarded Skank's ship, killing both him and the mutant octopus he thought was his mother (!)

Rico Dredd

First appearance: Prog #30
Dredd's clone-brother Rico was the only Cadet who could out-draw him, but his added flair came at a high cost – he had no respect for the law! After his return from 20 years on the penal colony of Titan, Rico wanted revenge, confronting Dredd at home and challenging him to a shootout. But Rico's time on Titan had slowed him just a fraction – all Dredd needed…

Murd the Oppressor

First appearance : Prog #170
Murd is a rarity amongst villains, in that he actually managed to kill Dredd! Vile, evil ruler of the planet Necros, he used Oracle Spice, taken from Sagbelly, a vast, mutant toad, to further his powers. Murd met his destiny when he revived Dredd so that he could feed him to Sagbelly–and ended up the main course!

MEET JUDGE DREDD...

Mega-City One, a vast 22nd century metropolis stretching down the eastern seaboard of post-apocalyptic North America. Beyond its walls lies the radioactive wasteland known as the Cursed Earth. As crime in the hugely overpopulated Mega-City runs rampant, only the judges can prevent total anarchy. Empowered to dispense instant justice, they are judge, jury and executioner in one — and the most feared and respected of them all is Judge Dredd. He *is* the law!

PREVIOUSLY...

Over the many years of his law enforcement career, Judge Dredd has had to deal with a multitude of villains, but there are a few who stand out from the rest: more evil, more powerful, more intelligent. These are the criminals who have pushed Dredd to the edge – until, of course, Dredd pushed back. Perhaps the most fearsome of these were the Dark Judges, – Death, Fear, Fire and Mortis – who developed the technology to cross from their own twisted dimension to Dredd's. The Dark Judges are gone – banished to limbo for all time – but that technology lives on…

GRUD, HOW I HATE THEM --

THEY'VE HAUNTED EVERY NIGHTMARE I'VE HAD SINCE I WAS OLD ENOUGH TO DREAM -- WITH THEIR POWER, WITH THEIR CRUELTY --

WITH THE **TERROR** THEY INSPIRE --

I KNEW THEY'D LEARN MY SECRETS, THE WAY THEY FIND OUT EVERYTHING -- I KNEW I WOULD BE **JUDGED** --

BUT NOT LIKE THIS!

NOT LIKE TONIGHT!

PROBE'S COMING IN.

THESE LATEST RESULTS ARE NOTHING SHORT OF REMARKABLE, KENZIE. THEY PROVE BEYOND THE SHADOW OF A DOUBT THAT YOU AND I SHOULD HAVE DINNER TONIGHT.

YOU KEEP THIS UP AND I CAN CALL IT **HARASSMENT**, KOHEN...

HOW CAN IT BE HARASSMENT WHEN YOU'RE THE BOSS?

HOLY DROKK-!

KILL THEM ALL! SANITISE!

EEEEEEEEEE!!

THANK DROKK!

AAAAAHH!

NO!

KENZIE—!

CONTROL, WE'RE IN THE WARP LAB, TECH 21! WE'VE GOT HER!

KOHEN!

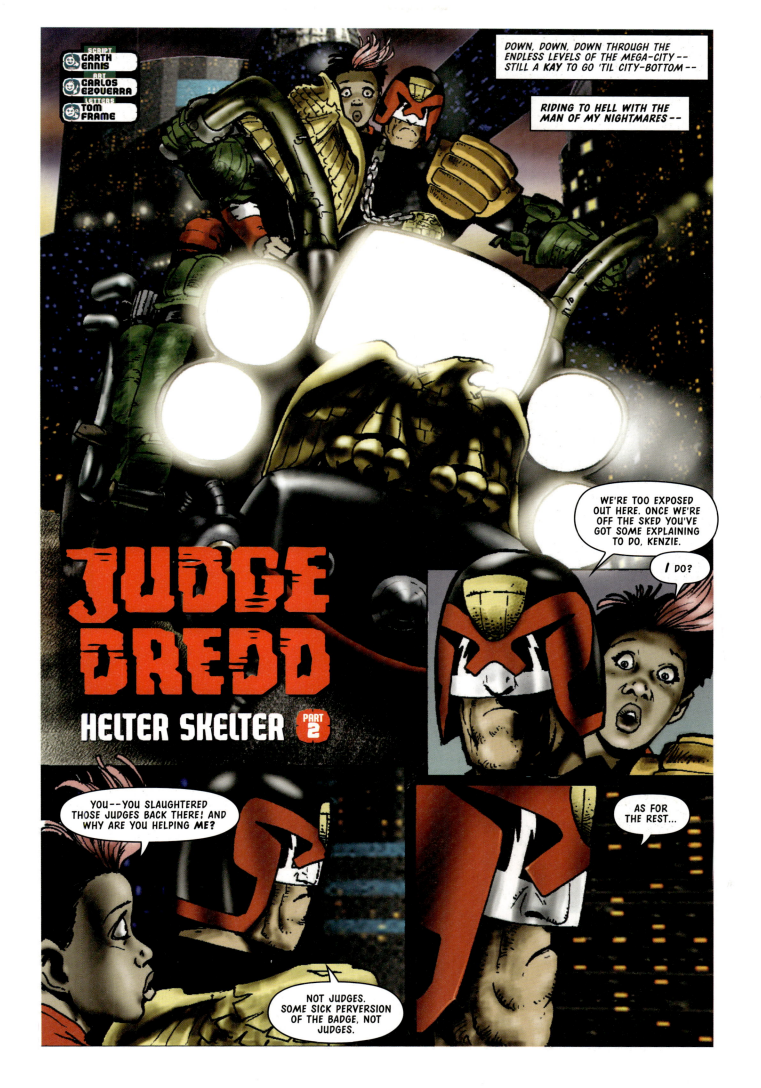

CALL-ME-KENNETH WILL *KRRRRZZZZTTT*

KRRRSSSHHHZZZZZTTTTT

CALL ME CALL ME CALL ME CALL ME

KRRZZZT! KRRZZZT! KRRZZZT!

SECURITY! ABOUT TIME YOU GOT HERE!

SO PUT ME ON REPORT, OLD MAN.

GIANT...?

IN HERE! WE'VE GOT HIM!

YOU'RE DEAD, GIANT. ORLOK SHOT YOU, RIGHT BEFORE THE APOCALYPSE WAR.

WHAT IS THIS?

IT WASN'T THE UNIFORM, OR THE GUN, OR THE OTHERS. IT WASN'T EVEN THE SMIRK ON HIS FACE.

THE GIANT I KNEW COULDN'T HAVE SURVIVED. COULDN'T HAVE GROWN OLD.

YOU THE ONE DEAD, OLD MAN. CHIEF JUDGE LET ME DO THE DEED A LONG TIME BACK. BEEN TOP DOG EVER SINCE.

HOW CAN *I* BE DEAD...?

IT WASN'T JUST CONTROL. I FLIPPED THROUGH THE CHANNELS-- SECURITY, TEK DIV, SATCOM, DORMS, THESE CREEPS WERE TAKING THE GRAND HALL APART.

THEY KNEW JUST WHERE TO HIT US--AND THEY JAMMED OUTGOING TRANSMISSIONS, TOO. NOT A SECTOR HOUSE IN THE CITY KNOWS WHAT'S HAPPENED.

ONE CHANNEL WAS STILL CLEAR--

BIKE! SOUTHSIDE EXIT! TO ME!

WILCO, JUDGE DREDD.

"I LISTENED IN ON THE BIKE RADIO--"

STRIKE TEAM ALPHA MOPPING UP! TEAM DELTA STILL MEETING RESISTANCE!

TEAM ECHO! CONTROL ROOM NULLIFIED!

OUTSTANDING, ECHO! SECURE THOSE TERMINALS, GET OUR UNITS TO TECH 21!

KENZIE'S THE KEY, REMEMBER! WE GET HER AND THERE'S NOT A DAMN THING THEY CAN DO ABOUT THIS!

GET DARIEN KENZIE AND THEIR CITY'S OURS!

WHICH BRINGS US UP TO DATE.

I LEFT THE GRAND HALL OF JUSTICE IN THE HANDS OF SCUM TO SAVE YOU, KENZIE. YOU'D BETTER HAVE BEEN WORTH IT.

NOW WHAT THE HELL IS GOING ON?

WE FIRST BECAME AWARE OF DIMENSION-JUMP TECHNOLOGY – OF THE VERY EXISTENCE OF OTHER DIMENSIONS – WITH THE COMING OF THE DARK JUDGES...

JUDGE DREDD

HELTER SKELTER PART 3

WE COULDN'T DUPLICATE THE MINIATURE DEVICES THEY USED, NOT WITH ANY MEASURE OF SUCCESS -- SO WE BUILT ONE BIG DIMENSION JUMP AND ANCHORED IT IN THE WARP LAB AT TECH 21.

THE OBVIOUS DANGER OF THE DARK JUDGES, ALONG WITH WHATEVER ELSE MIGHT BE OUT THERE, LED TO THE USE OF ROBOT PROBES FOR OUR RESEARCH. NOTHING ORGANIC WOULD GO THROUGH – AND ANYTHING COMING BACK WITH THE PROBE WOULD BE FRIED WHITE-HOT BY THE FAILSAFE CIRCUITRY...

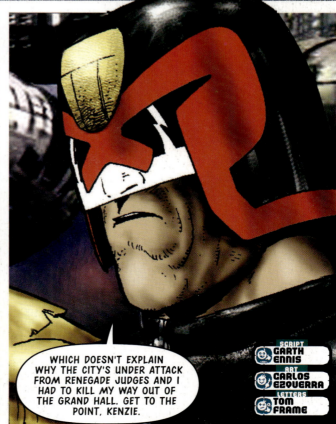

WHICH DOESN'T EXPLAIN WHY THE CITY'S UNDER ATTACK FROM RENEGADE JUDGES AND I HAD TO KILL MY WAY OUT OF THE GRAND HALL. GET TO THE POINT, KENZIE.

SCRIPT
GARTH ENNIS
ART
CARLOS EZQUERRA
LETTERS
TOM FRAME

SOMETHING'S WRONG, IS WHAT I'M TRYING TO SAY. WE SHOULD HAVE DETECTED THE GRAND HALL INCURSION AT TECH 21, WE'VE GOT THE GEAR TO DO IT -- JUST LIKE THE FAILSAFES SHOULD HAVE TAKEN CARE OF THE GEEKS THAT CAME BACK WITH THE LATEST PROBE.

SOMETHING'S WRONG, AND I THINK I KNOW WHAT IT IS...

I THINK WE'VE GOT WHAT I CALL HELTER-SKELTER.

YOU DO, HUH?

LOOK, I'VE BEEN RUNNING THE WARP LAB AT '21 FOR FOUR YEARS NOW. I'M THE YOUNGEST TEK GRAD EVER TO HOLD THE POST -- SO DO ME THE COURTESY OF TAKING ME SERIOUSLY, WILL YOU?

THERE ARE THOUSANDS OF ALTERNATE DIMENSIONS AND MILLIONS OF EMPTY ONES -- ALL SEPARATE, BUT ALL ACCESSIBLE FROM THE OTHERS BY MEANS OF DIMENSION WARP.

THE THING IS, ONCE YOU START JUMPING BETWEEN THEM YOU'RE MESSING WITH THE VERY FABRIC OF REALITY ITSELF. IT'S LIKE A VERY, VERY DELICATE WEB -- PUT TOO MUCH STRESS ON ONE STRAND AND YOU WEAKEN A DOZEN OTHERS. THE DARK JUDGES' JUMPING BACK AND FORTH HASN'T HELPED, HELL, SOMETIMES I WONDER ABOUT OUR OWN RESEARCH...

BUT WORST OF ALL WAS THE APOCALYPSE WARP.

THE SOVS' DIMENSION SHIELD? FROM THE WAR?

ALL HAIL THE CHIEF JUDGE!

WELCOME -- SSRRP! CHIEF JUDGE!

I HOPE YOUR -- SSRRP! TRIP ACROSS THE -- SSRRP! DIMENSION WARP WAS -- SSRRP!

LATER FOR THAT, LACKEY! REPORT!

WE HOLD NINETY PERCENT OF THEIR GRAND HALL, CHIEF JUDGE. SOME UNITS MEETING RESISTANCE ON THE LOWER FLOORS. OUTGOING TRANSMISSIONS JAMMED.

DREDD?

UH... ESCAPED...

I'D BE DISAPPOINTED IN HIM IF HE HADN'T. THAT LUDICROUS ROBOT, AND GIANT SOMEWHAT PAST HIS BEST... NO MATTER, THERE'LL BE TIME ENOUGH FOR DREDD.

AND THIS?

THEIR CHIEF JUDGE. WE WARPED THE KENNETH DROID IN RIGHT ON TOP OF HER -- SHARED THE SAME SPACE-TIME ALMOST A TENTH OF A SECOND. MASSIVE PSYCHOLOGICAL SHOCK.

SHE AIN'T SEEN NOTHING YET.

FIRST THINGS FIRST: WE CAN'T HAVE THE GALLANT DEFENDERS DOWNSTAIRS ALERTING THE OTHER SECTORS. GET ME AN OPEN CHANNNEL.

WE'LL SEE WHAT A FEW WELL-CHOSEN WORDS CAN DO...!

...EVEN THE CIVILIAN CHANNELS ARE SCRAMBLED.

THIS HELTER-SKELTER THEORY -- YOU'RE SURE THAT'S WHAT WE'VE GOT HERE?

THE GEEKS I MENTIONED -- THE OTHER JUDGES MASSACRED THEM ON SIGHT. SO THEIR ARRIVAL WASN'T DELIBERATE, THEY WERE JUST SNAGGED BY THE DISRUPTION FROM THE JUDGES' WARP. ARRIVED AT TECH 21 BECAUSE ITS SIGNAL IS STRONGER THAN OUR BAD GUYS' EQUIPMENT.

SPILLING OVER, SEE? WHAT YOU DON'T WANT BROUGHT OVER ALONG WITH WHAT YOU DO.

THAT RIGHT THERE IS HELTER-SKELTER.

SO WHY DO THESE CREEPS THINK YOU'RE SO IMPORTANT?

WELL, THEY SEEM TO HAVE DONE THEIR RESEARCH, THEY KNOW YOUR SET-UP INSIDE-OUT. THEY MUST KNOW I RUN THE WARP LAB.

NO-ONE ELSE UNDERSTANDS THE TECHNOLOGY LIKE I DO, NOT BEYOND A THEORETICAL LEVEL. NO-ONE ELSE KNOWS HOW TO STOP THE DISRUPTION...

HOW TO STABILISE... THE WARP...

OH MY GRUD.

YOU'RE GOING TO KILL ME.

WHAT?

YOU ARE! YOU-YOU THINK THEY CAN'T DO THIS WITHOUT ME! YOU'RE GOING TO SHOOT ME SO THEY CAN'T MAKE ME HELP THEM -- HELP BRING MORE OF THEIR PEOPLE ACROSS!

OH GRUD, YOU JUDGES, PEOPLE'S LIVES ARE NOTHING TO YOU! I'M JUST AN ASSET THAT YOUR ENEMY CAN USE, AND NOW YOU'RE GOING TO KILL ME!

I KNEW THIS WOULD HAPPEN! I ALWAYS DROKKING KNEW IT!

DON'T BE STUPID, KENZIE. YOU'RE A CITIZEN OF MEGA-CITY ONE AND I'M SWORN TO PROTECT YOU.

I'M GOING TO TRY TO MAKE THE SECTOR LINE, GET WORD OUT TO THE CITY. YOU'D BETTER STICK WITH ME; IT SOUNDS LIKE OUR TEKS ARE GOING TO NEED YOU --

ALERT - ALERT -

TWIN CONTACTS CLOSING ON THIS UNIT -- H-WAGON CLASS -- ALERT - ALERT -

GET ON THE BIKE, KENZIE.

B-B-BUT--

ON THE BIKE.

JUDGE DREDD
HELTER SKELTER PART 4

HOLD THE GRAND HALL!

SCRIPT
GARTH ENNIS

ART
CARLOS EZQUERRA

LETTERS
TOM FRAME

POUR IT ON, BOYS! GIVE THESE SCUMBAGS THE OLD MEGA-CITY HELLO!

KOBIE, THERE'S TOO MANY OF THEM!

THEY'VE TAKEN THE UPPER FLOORS, THE WAGON BAYS! THEY'VE EVEN GOT CONTROL!

THE HELL WITH 'EM! SON, I'VE BEEN A JUDGE THESE THIRTY YEARS, AND I AIN'T RUNNING FROM ANYONE!

GIVE 'EM HELL!!

JUDGES OF MEGA-CITY ONE!

AAAH -!

DO YOU REMEMBER?

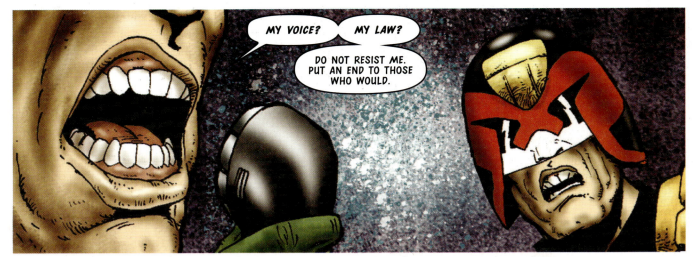

CHIEF JUDGE, THEY-THEY'RE TURNING ON EACH OTHER! THEY'RE WIPING EACH OTHER OUT, ALL OVER THE BUILDING!

HOW DID YOU--

OLD TRICK.

VERY OLD TRICK.

CHECK THE SURVIVORS CAREFULLY. ANY OF THEIR JUDGES WITH LESS THAN TWENTY-FIVE YEARS' SERVICE - EXECUTE THEM.

WHAT NEWS OF DREDD?

WE SCRAMBLED H-WAGONS AS SOON AS WE TOOK THEIR HANGARS, CHIEF JUDGE. CONTROL HAS THEM PATROLLING THE SECTOR LINE.

BUT...BRINGING THE CREWS ACROSS SO SOON AFTER OUR ASSAULT UNITS - IT'S PUTTING A HELL OF A STRAIN ON THE WARP, AND OUR TEKS CAN'T STABILISE THE CONNECTION. WE NEED THE KENZIE WOMAN...

HAVEN'T OUR JUDGES BROUGHT HER BACK FROM TECH 21?

WE FOUND THEIR BODIES, CHIEF JUDGE.

WE THINK, UH... WE THINK DREDD HAS DARIEN KENZIE...

WELL THAT DOES NOT PLEASE ME, LACKEY, THAT IS NOT VERY GOOD NEWS AT ALL--

CHIEF JUDGE FROM CONTROL!

WAGON FLIGHT DELTA REPORTS LONE JUDGE SIGHTED, HEADING FOR SECTOR TWO! JUDGE BELIEVED TO BE DREDD!

WAGONS IN PURSUIT!

AAAAAHH! AAAAAAAHHH! OH MY GRUD, THEY'RE GOING TO *KILL US!!*

THOSE ARE WARNING SHOTS, KENZIE. THEY WANT YOU ALIVE, REMEMBER?

DROKK IT, DO YOU HAVE TO HOLD SO TIGHT--?

YES!!

DELTA TWO FROM DELTA ONE, WATCH IT, YOU'RE GETTING WAY TOO CLOSE--

ONE FROM TWO, WE CAN'T LET HIM MAKE THE SECTOR LINE! COME ON, WHAT CAN HE--

ARMOUR PIERCING!

CAN'T SAY I'M SURPRISED--

NOT OUR TWENTIETH.

NOT OUR EARTH.

HELTER SKELTER?

IT'S REALLY KICKING IN NOW, IF THINGS LIKE THAT ARE SHOWING UP. AND THE MORE THESE GUYS USE THE WARP, THE WORSE IT'S GOING TO GET...

THAT MAY BE THE LEAST OF OUR WORRIES.

SOMETHING GIANT TOLD ME - SOMETHING I CAN'T STOP THINKING ABOUT.

THE CHIEF JUDGE LET HIM KILL ME, HE SAID. THAT HAPPENED IN THIS DIMENSION TOO, A LONG TIME AGO. THE GIANT I KNEW WAS FAKING, BUYING TIME TO ESCAPE...

BUT - YES, IT FITS. THE CHIEF JUDGE LET HIM DO IT.

CHIEF JUDGE CAL.

JUDGE DREDD

HELTER SKELTER PART 5

ALL CITIZENS, DISPERSE AND RETURN TO YOUR HOMES! THE SITUATION HAS BEEN NORMALISED!

DROKKIN' THING JUST CAME OUTTA NOWHERE! JUST-- APPEARED!

DAMN NEAR KILLED US ALL BEFORE THE H-WAGONS GOT IT!

SCRIPT
GARTH ENNIS

ART
CARLOS EZQUERRA

LETTERS
TOM FRAME

RETURN TO OUR HOMES-? THERE'S A GIANT SPUGGIN' MONSTER WRAPPED AROUND THE BLOCK!

AND PEOPLE ARE HURT IN THERE, JUDGE! WHERE ARE THE RESCUE TEAMS? WHERE ARE THE MED-WAGONS?

EVERYTHING IS UNDER CONTROL! DISPERSE! WE WILL NOT HESITATE TO USE ULTIMATE FORCE!

IF THEY HARM ONE SINGLE CITIZEN -

I'LL SHOW THEM ULTIMATE FORCE.

CROWD'S BREAKING UP...

YOU KNOW WHAT THAT IS OUT THERE? THAT'S THE **TITAN OF PEEM**, NATIVE TO THE KOOKARATCH SYSTEM. THAT SOMETHING THAT SIZE COULD GET PULLED ACROSS THE DIMENSIONS, MY GRUD...

YOUR **HELTER SKELTER** EFFECT AGAIN, KENZIE?

YOU SAY THAT LIKE I STARTED IT.

BUT YES. AND IF THESE PHONEY JUDGES THINK THEY CAN KEEP A LID ON IT, THEY AIN'T SEEN NOTHING YET.

BIKE'S MONITORING DEPARTMENT COMS--

GRAND HALL FROM SECTOR HOUSE FOUR-- MORE REPORTS OF, AH, **PHENOMENA** FROM UNITS OBSERVING YOUR SECTOR--

LOCALISED ANOMALIES, FOUR. WEATHER CONTROL SAYS WE CAN COPE.

GRAND HALL, YOU'RE SURE YOU DON'T NEED ASSIST--

KEEP ALL UNITS ON PATROL LINES, FOUR. THAT'S DIRECT FROM CHIEF JUDGE HERSHEY.

THAT'S FROM **CAL.**

THEY MUST FIGURE THEY CAN FIND ME BEFORE THE DISRUPTION GOES CRITICAL. THE IDIOTS COULD LOSE THIS WORLD AND THEIR OWN ALONG WITH IT.

I THINK I SHOULD SURRENDER-- AT LEAST THEN I CAN STABILISE THE WARP.

AND THE NEXT THING THEY'LL DO IS HAVE YOU BRING OVER THEIR ARMY.

NO DICE.

BUT BY THE TIME WE GET ACROSS THE SECTOR LINE FOR HELP--

CHANGE OF PLAN.

SO LONG AS THESE CREEPS HOLD THE GRAND HALL, THEY CAN KILL THE PHONES AND RADIO -- LOCK DOWN THE SECTOR WITH SPYCAMS -- VECTOR EVERY UNIT THEY'VE GOT ONTO ANYONE TRYING TO MAKE IT OUT.

WE CAN'T AFFORD TO WAIT FOR NIGHTFALL. WE NEED TO CLOSE THIS DOWN NOW, BEFORE THE CITY GOES TO HELL. SO WE MAKE THE RUN THEY'RE NOT EXPECTING --

WE GO FOR TECH 21.

YOU STABILISE THE WARP FROM THERE AND STOP THE DISRUPTION. I RIG THE WARP LAB WITH HI-EX.

WHAT...?

AS SOON AS CAL GETS CONFIDENT ENOUGH TO BRING HIS MAIN FORCE OVER, I BLOW THE WHOLE PLACE TO HELL.

BUT THAT'S MONSTROUS!

IT'S SENSE. WE TAKE OUT THE BULK OF THE OPPOSITION AND THEIR MEANS OF COMING BACK THROUGH OUR OWN FACILITY.

AND OUR MEANS OF EVER REACHING ANOTHER DIMENSION AGAIN! EVERYTHING WE'VE GOT IS AT TECH 21 -- OUR RESEARCH, OUR BLUEPRINTS, EVEN THE OTHER DARK JUDGES' D-JUMPS WE BASED OUR OWN ON!

DESTROY THE PLACE NOW AND YOU'RE CUTTING US OFF FROM THOUSANDS OF WORLDS! FROM EVERYTHING WE CAN LEARN FROM THEM!

HAVEN'T BEEN MUCH HELP SO FAR.

THERE HAS TO BE ANOTHER WAY! I CAN'T BE A PART OF THIS! I WON'T!

DARIEN KENZIE.

I KNOW YOU.

DEMOCRACY NOW FUNDRAISER ABOUT TWO YEARS AGO. YOU SPOKE AT IT. YOU'RE LISTED ON THE STEERING COMMITTEE.

YOU'RE A DEM.

SO WHAT? IT'S NOT ILLEGAL, IS IT?

NOT IN AND OF ITSELF. BUT JOINING WHISPER OF FREEDOM, OR THE MAILER LEGACY, ONE OF THE MILITANT GROUPS -- THAT'S A DEFINITE NO-NO.

YOU DONE ANYTHING THAT STUPID?

GRUD, YOU JUDGES --! YOU NEVER CHANGE, DO YOU? EVEN NOW YOU'RE PARANOID ABOUT THE TINIEST THREAT TO YOUR PRECIOUS POWER!

ALL YOU DO IS PRY, AND INTERROGATE, AND THREATEN --

YEAH?

WHO WAS IT SAVED YOUR LIFE LAST NIGHT, THEN? OTTO SUMP?

GROW UP, KENZIE.

YOU'LL DO AS YOU'RE TOLD.

CHIEF JUDGE HERSHEY! FEELING BETTER NOW, I HOPE?

YOU WON'T GET AWAY WITH THIS, MONSTER. WHATEVER INSANITY IT IS YOU'RE UP TO.

WON'T I REALLY?

THOSE AREN'T **MY** JUDGES HOLDING YOU, YOU KNOW.

SUBLIMINAL CONTROL. SAME WAY YOU SEIZED POWER THE LAST TIME.

DIFFERENT CAL, SAME TRICK.

YOUR YOUNGER JUDGES WOULDN'T REMEMBER MY VOICE, OF COURSE. WHICH IS WHY I HAD TO KILL EVERY SINGLE ONE OF THEM ON THE GRAND HALL STAFF.

YOU — DISGUSTING VERMIN—!

YOU WERE STILL AT THE ACADEMY THEN TOO, WEREN'T YOU?

WHATEVER AM I GOING TO DO WITH YOU...?

CHIEF JUDGE!

WHAT **IS** IT, LACKEY?

NEXT GROUP WARPING OVER NOW, CHIEF JUDGE! HERE THEY COME!

INDEED.

YOU SHOULD WATCH THIS, MY DEAR. IT MIGHT GIVE YOU AN INKLING OF WHAT THIS CITY OF YOURS IS IN FOR.

WHAT...?

WE STOPPED FOR NOTHING. TECH 21 OR BUST. THE ENEMY HAD WOKEN UP TO WHAT THEY'D CAUSED - WAY, **WAY** TOO LATE.

TRY AS THEY MIGHT TO STOP IT, THEY WERE STUCK ON THE HELTER SKELTER.

SCRIPT
GARTH ENNIS
ART
CARLOS EZQUERRA
LETTERS
TOM FRAME

BY NOW THE BIKE RADIO WAS PICKING UP ALL KINDS OF STUFF - FRAGMENTS OF TRANSMISSIONS FROM WHEN AND WHEREVER, FILTERED ACROSS THE DIMENSION WARP...

WHERE WILL YOU GO?

OUT.

GOODBYE, RODICE.

ENEMY SUICIDE SQUAD ON DARK SIDE OF THE MOON, CRATER GAUSS ON THE WIDE SEA! *VAPE 'EM, VCs - VAPE 'EM!*

LOSS OF HYPER-POWER 99%—100% CONCLUSION: MACH ONE TERMINATED! NOW CLOSING DOWN TRANSMISSION--

...WE'LL ALWAYS BE **ONE UP** ON SCUM LIKE YOU! YOU'RE **FILTH**, EDVARK - THE BATTLEFIELD'S A CLEANER PLACE THAN MILLI-COM'LL EVER BE!

IT WAS ALL THE FURY AND TERROR AND SADNESS OF A THOUSAND DIFFERENT WORLDS.

I'LL NEVER BE ABLE TO FORGET IT.

BEEN NICE KNOWIN' YA, GOOD BUDDIES. GUESS THIS IS IT.

TRUCK TUCKER, Y'HEAR?

JUDGE DREDD

HELTER SKELTER PART **6**

CAL, WHAT THE HELL ARE **THEY** DOING HERE?

OH, THAT'S JUST THE LOCALS. SOME TWO DOZEN JUDGES — ALL AT LEAST TWENTY-FIVE-YEAR MEN, ALL UNDER MY CONTROL. AND CHIEF JUDGE HERSHEY, WHO SADLY ISN'T.

WHATEVER SHALL WE DO WITH THEM, DO YOU THINK?

WAR MARSHAL KAZAN?

EXECUTE THEM AND HAVE DONE WITH IT. WE HAVE MORE PRESSING MATTERS TO ATTEND TO.

DON UGGIE APELINO?

NUTS TA THAT! MAKE 'EM **SUFFER,** THE SCHMUCKS!

GRAMPUS?

ALL THE SAME TO HUNGRY KLEGG! EAT 'EM!

FINK ANGEL?

DIBS ON THE WUMMAN, GRAMPUS!

CAPTAIN SKANK?

GIVE 'EM TO THE SHARKS, MATEY! *ZZZZT!* WE'LL LAUGH AS THE SEAS BOIL RED WI' THEIR BLOOD!

RICO DREDD?

GIVE THEM TO ME.

GIVE ALL THE JUDGES TO ME.

MURD THE OPPRESSOR?

GIVE THEM... TO ME.

I HAVE AN OLDER WAY IN MIND.

THAT SOUNDS RATHER PROMISING...!

LET HIM GET ON WITH IT, WHATEVER IT IS! THE PLAN, CAL! WHY ARE WE SO FAR BEHIND SCHEDULE?

DARIEN KENZIE IS STILL AT LARGE. HER CAPTURE IS ONLY A MATTER OF TIME.

WE DO NOT **HAVE** TIME-!

WE NEED THAT WOMAN TO HELP US USE THE WARP WITH SAFETY. HER UNDERSTANDING, THE LEVEL OF TECHNOLOGY SHE WORKS ON - THEY ARE YEARS AHEAD OF OUR OWN.

MY OWN, KAZAN. MY TEKS, MY D-JUMP... MY FORCE OF JUDGES, COME TO THAT...

AND **MY** PLAN!

PROPERLY EXECUTED, IT WILL YIELD OUR TRIUMPH! MISTIMED OR MISHANDLED, IT WILL DOOM US ALL!

FIND HER!!

GGGRRRRRRRRRRRR

JUDGE DREDD

HELTER SKELTER PART 7

GGGRRAAAAARRRR

AAAAAAIIIIEEEII

RUN!

NAIN! NAIN!

SCRIPT
GARTH ENNIS

ART
CARLOS EZQUERRA

LETTERS
TOM FRAME

THEY'RE PANICKING!

NOT THE IDEA AT ALL, DROKK IT! I WANTED THAT ONE-EYED HAG KEPT OCCUPIED!

BIKE CANNON - MINIMUM ELEVATION!

BUDDA BUDDA

WHAT-- AAAH!

AAAARRGGHH!

BUDDA BUDDA

EEEEIIIGGHH!

CR-CRAWL FOR IT~!

NOOOOOO!!

NNOOOOOOAAAAARRRRGGGHH!!

THAT'S A BIT MORE LIKE IT...

AAAAAIIIIEEEEEEEEEEEE

TECH 21 AHEAD! WHICH WAY TO THE WARP LAB, KENZIE?

LEVEL TWO - BUT LISTEN, THIS IS WHERE ALL THIS CHAOS IS CENTERED! THERE'S NO TELLING WHAT MIGHT BE IN HERE--

DUDE!

YOU SEE MY POINT!

WHAT I FOUND IN THERE WAS SOMETHING **WORSE**--

I'VE DONE WHAT I CAN TO MINIMISE DISRUPTION, BUT IF THEY KEEP ON USING THEIR OWN EQUIPMENT...

UH... WHAT IS THAT, EXACTLY?

HALF A KILO OF THERMEX, PART OF THE LAWMASTER'S SECURITY SYSTEM - COMPUTER CAN SET IT OFF IF THE BIKE FALLS INTO THE WRONG HANDS.

SHOULD BE ENOUGH TO TAKE OUT THE LAB TWICE OVER.

ONCE CAL TRIES WARPING HIS MAIN FORCE ACROSS I'LL DETONATE IT BY REMOTE...

OH GRUD, YOU'RE REALLY GOING THROUGH WITH THIS! YOU'RE GOING TO DESTROY EVERYTHING WE WORKED FOR HERE, EVERYTHING WE TRIED TO ACHIEVE!

NO OTHER WAY, KENZIE.

YOU BLOW UP THE WARP LAB AND ANY CHANCE WE'VE GOT OF REACHING ANOTHER DIMENSION IS GONE FOREVER!

THERE'S SO MUCH OUT THERE THAT WE CAN EXPLORE, AND STUDY, AND LEARN FROM! THERE ARE WORLDS WHERE THEY'VE CURED EVERY DISEASE IN EXISTENCE! WHERE THEY'VE BEEN AT PEACE FOR HUNDREDS AND HUNDREDS OF YEARS!

AND EVEN BEYOND THAT, THERE ARE PEOPLE AND CULTURES AND PLACES **BEYOND YOUR IMAGINATION!** SO WILD YOU CAN ONLY MARVEL AT THE **WONDER** OF IT ALL - SO **INCREDIBLE** YOU CAN HARDLY EVEN FIT IT IN YOUR HEAD!

NO OTHER WAY.

LET'S GO.

DO... DO YOU KNOW THE THINGS I'VE SEEN OUT THERE?

DO YOU KNOW HOW MANY OTHER WORLDS THERE **ARE**?

YOU'RE GOING TO HAVE TO. WHEN THE TIME COMES, I WON'T HESITATE TO BLOW THIS PLACE TO PIECES.

YOU'D BETTER TAG ALONG, KENZIE. CAL MUST HAVE HIS OWN D-JUMP GEAR AT THE GRAND HALL – I MAY NEED YOU TO HELP CLOSE THINGS DOWN AT THAT END.

LOOKS LIKE SHE'S GORGED HERSELF. MUST BE SLEEPING IT OFF.

ALL THE SAME--

SILENT RUNNING, BIKE. LIGHTS OFF.

WILCO, JUDGE DREDD.

AND OFF WE WENT TO DESTROY EVERYTHING I HELD DEAR.

MY MIND WAS SPINNING WITH THE HORROR OF IT. I COULDN'T LET HIM DO THIS. I SIMPLY COULDN'T.

BUT HOW WOULD I EVER STOP HIM...?

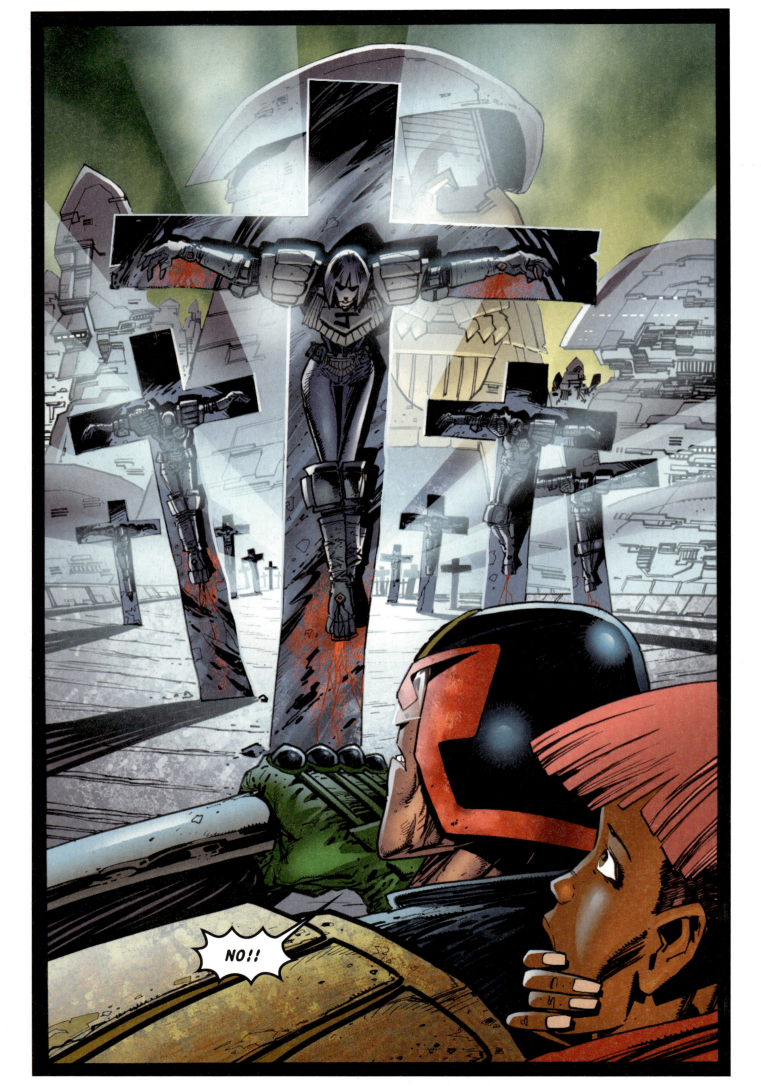

SCRIPT
GARTH ENNIS

ART
CARLOS EZQUERRA

LETTERS
ELLIE DE VILLE

JUDGE DREDD
HELTER SKELTER PART 10

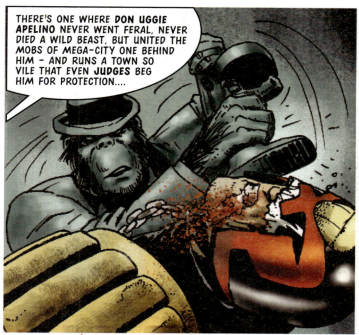

THERE'S ONE WHERE **DON UGGIE APELINO** NEVER WENT FERAL, NEVER DIED A WILD BEAST, BUT UNITED THE MOBS OF MEGA-CITY ONE BEHIND HIM - AND RUNS A TOWN SO VILE THAT EVEN **JUDGES** BEG HIM FOR PROTECTION....

ONE WHERE **FINK ANGEL** SURVIVED THE PA ANGEL SUPER SCREAM TORTURE MACHINE, AND LED A CURSED EARTH **MUTANT ARMY** TO BURN THE HATED MEGA-CITY TO THE GROUND...

ONE WHERE **CAPTAIN SKANK** WAS NOT SOME EAST-MEG STOOGE, BUT RULES THE **BLACK ATLANTIC** AS ITS PIRATE KING -

ZZZZZTTTT

OOPS-A-DAISY! GOODBYE, SAILOR!

WATCH HIM, YOU FOOLS!

WELL, OKAY, THEN.

SCRATCH THAT LAST ONE.

I'M SURE YOU GET THE IDEA.

YOU'RE DEAD ON THE WORLDS WE COME FROM. WE BEAT YOU.

WE SHOT YOU AND LYNCHED YOU, AND STABBED YOU AND DROWNED YOU, AND TORTURED AND POISONED YOU...

AND WE WERE TRIUMPHANT...

AND YOU LOST.

SO IMAGINE HOW WE FELT WHEN OLD MURD HERE, WHOSE NECROMANCY LETS HIM SEE ACROSS DIMENSIONS, CAME TO EACH OF US IN TURN AND SAID —

HE LIVES, MY FRIENDS.

THERE'S A WORLD OUT THERE WHERE DREDD WON.

AND WE COULDN'T STAND IT. THE THOUGHT OF A WORLD WHERE YOU'D BEATEN US, YOU'D **KILLED US** - OUR ALTERNATE SELVES ON YOUR WORLD, YES, BUT IT WAS STILL MORE THAN WE COULD STOMACH...

I HAD MY TEKS RUSH THROUGH PROTOTYPE D-JUMP TECHNOLOGY, AND BROUGHT THIS LITTLE BAND TOGETHER, AND READIED MY JUDGES FOR THE ASSAULT -

AND I DEVISED THE PLAN THAT WOULD DELIVER US OUR PRIZE:

YOU.

YOU HATEFUL...

MURDERING...

SELF-RIGHTEOUS...

SPOILSPORT...

NAZI...

BUTCHER.

THAT'S WHAT THIS HAS BEEN ABOUT. THAT'S WHAT WE'RE HERE FOR.

YOU.

SO YOU CROSS TO THIS DIMENSION AND RISK THE LIVES OF BILLIONS - TO TAKE YOUR REVENGE ON A MAN YOU'VE EACH ALREADY MURDERED?

SMALL WONDER I KILLED YOU MANIACS THE FIRST TIME.

HELL, DREDD -

YA JUST DON'T KNOW WHUT IT'S LIKE TA HATE YA.

THIS IS THE D-JUMP UNIT OUR TEKS WARPED ACROSS TO US. IT'S NOT AS SOPHISTICATED AS YOUR OWN EQUIPMENT, BUT IT'S ENOUGH TO DO THE JOB.

I-I'M NOT GOING TO DO THIS! I REFUSE!

SO YOU CAN WITHSTAND TORTURE, THEN? MY JUDGES CAN BEAT AND BURN AND SKIN AWAY, AND YOU'RE GOING TO HOLD OUT?

LISTEN. **PLEASE LISTEN.** THE LEVEL OF PRECISION YOU WANT HERE, IT **CAN'T** BE ACHIEVED WITH THE DIMENSION WARP.

IF I TRY THIS I'LL DAMN A DOZEN WORLDS TO CHAOS AND HORROR, AND I MEAN **FOREVER.** I MEAN AWFUL, TWISTING TORMENT FOR ALL OF US, STUCK ON THE HELTER SKELTER FOR ETERNITY...

COME, NOW. YOU'RE THE EXPERT.

I'M SURE YOU'VE GOT THE MAGIC TOUCH.

AH...WAR MARSHAL KAZAN WANTED TO BE HERE FOR THIS, CHIEF JUDGE. I SHOULD GO AND FETCH HIM, HE REALLY WAS MOST INSISTENT...

YOU ACTUALLY ARE AS STUPID AS YOU LOOK, AREN'T YOU, LACKEY? DO YOU THINK I CAME ALL THE WAY FROM ANOTHER DIMENSION TO SHARE THIS CITY WITH SOME SOVIET OIK?

I'LL DEAL WITH KAZAN WHEN THE TIME COMES. HIM AND THE REST OF THAT RABBLE, COLOURFUL THOUGH THEY MAY BE.

GET THE GIRL TO WORK, LACKEY. ANY MORE HEARTFELT PLEAS FOR SANITY--

ONE EAR, ONE EYE.

IT'S

IT'S IN MY

HEAD UNNHH!!

GRUD ROT YOUR SOUL...

COLDEST... MEANEST...SON OF A...

HHHHH

SOMETHING IN THE BLOOD.

ALL SYSTEMS UP. D-JUMP READY FOR ENABLING.

OH, GRUD...

OH, GOOD.

THE LINK TO MY HOME DIMENSION IS PRE-SET. MY JUDGES ARE STANDING BY.

BRING SIX SQUADS OVER FOR STARTERS -- SOUNDS LIKE DREDD'S WIPED THE FLOOR WITH THAT CIRCUS IN THERE. THEN KEEP PILING ON THE PRESSURE, PUSH THE WARP UNTIL THE TWO WORLDS BLUR --

AND CLOSE IT DOWN WHEN MEGA-CITY ONE IS MINE.

B-B-BUT--

NOW.

OH NO!

OH THANK GRUD!

LACKEY, DO YOUR DROKKING DUTY--

SCRIPT
GARTH ENNIS
ART
CARLOS EZQUERRA
LETTERS
TOM FRAME

AT ONCE, CHIEF JUDGE!

THE D-JUMP, WOMAN! REVERSE THE LINK!

GLADLY I GIVE MY LIFE FOR MY —

AAAAAH!

STOMM!!

JUDGE DREDD
HELTER SKELTER PART 12

IT'S LOCKED ON HIS HOMEWORLD!

STAND CLEAR--

HI-EX!!

TELL ME THAT WAS ENOUGH...

TO BREAK THE LINK, STOP HIM GETTING HOME -- SURE.

BUT HE'LL STILL GET OUT OF THE WARP. ANY D-JUMP LOCAL TO HIS DEPARTURE DIMENSION WILL AUTOMATICALLY PULL HIM IN.

THE NEAREST IS...TECH 21.

HE CAN USE THE EQUIPMENT THERE TO GET HOME.

HE COULD IF IT WASN'T WIRED WITH THERMEX. DETONATOR'S GOOD FOR A TEN-KAY RADIUS --

WHAT THE HELL-?

WELL, WELL.

YOU'LL BE SEEING ME AGAIN, DREDD.

A LOT SOONER THAN YOU—

ALL OUR RESEARCH.

ALL OUR WORK.

ANY CHANCE WE HAD OF REACHING ALL THOSE WORLDS.

...SOMETHING YOU WANT TO TELL ME?

LIFTED IT FROM YOUR BELT JUST AFTER YOU FOUND THE CHIEF JUDGE. YOU MUST HAVE HAD TOO MUCH ON YOUR MIND.

HAD THIS IDEA ABOUT SAVING THE WARP LAB, FINDING A WAY TO FIX THINGS WITHOUT DESTROYING EVERYTHING WE'D DONE... BUT WITH CAL ON THE LOOSE...

WELL.

SO WHAT ABOUT YOUR TWO THOUSAND WORLDS?

...

I GUESS I'LL JUST HAVE TO IMAGINE THEM.

LET'S GO, KENZIE.

NO-ONE ELSE CROSSED OVER FROM CAL'S DIMENSION, OR FROM ANY OF THE OTHERS. WHEN NONE OF THEIR PEOPLE RETURNED FROM MEGA-CITY ONE THEY PROBABLY GOT THE MESSAGE.

CHIEF JUDGE HERSHEY RECOVERED QUICKLY. SHE GAVE IMMEDIATE PRIORITY TO ELIMINATING ALL RESIDUALS FROM THE CRISIS, THE NORTS AND GEEKS AND SO ON -- THOUGH NOTHING WAS EVER SEEN OF THE VAMPIRE SOLDIERS, OR EVEN THE BIG TYRANNOSAUR.

THEY'RE OUT THERE NOW, I GUESS, MAYBE EVEN HOME -- SWEPT BACK BY THE DISRUPTION THAT BROUGHT THEM HERE.

CAL'S JUDGES WERE HUNTED WITHOUT RESPITE. THOSE WHO RESISTED PERISHED...

THOSE WHO SURRENDERED --

AFTERWARDS, PSI-DIVISION AND OTHER PSYCHICS REPORTED ASSOCIATED PHENOMENA FOR YEARS. CHIEF AMONG THESE -- AND MOST PERSISTENT -- WAS CAL.

OFFICIALLY HE DIED AT TECH 21 -- BUT TO THIS DAY, DREAMS AND VISIONS ARE LOGGED OF A GHOSTLY FIGURE TRAPPED IN THE VOID BETWEEN THE WORLDS, HOWLING WITH INSANITY, TEARING AT HIS EYES IN TORMENT --

RIDING THE HELTER SKELTER FOREVER.

A WORD OF ADVICE, KENZIE.

ANY EXTREMIST LITERATURE YOUR DEM FRIENDS MIGHT HAVE LEFT WITH YOU -- BE A GOOD IDEA TO GET RID OF IT.

WHAT...?

YOU GET SOME HOTSHOT ROOKIE WORKING A 59D, THAT'S EXACTLY THE KIND OF THING HE'D BE OUT TO IMPRESS HIS EXAMINER WITH.

I -- UH --

THIS IS YOU.

AN DURY BLOCK

WHY DID YOU SURRENDER TO CAL AND HIS MONSTERS?

THEY WERE GOING TO KILL YOU.

BUT IT WAS SUCH A MASSIVE RISK...! I MEAN IF THEY'D KILLED YOU, CAL WOULD'VE BEEN FREE TO DO WHATEVER HE WANTED!

I FIGURED I COULD TAKE 'EM.

YOU CALLED THE JUDGES A PRIVILIGED ELITE, KENZIE. YOU WERE RIGHT. WE ARE AN ELITE.

THERE IS A PRIVILEGE.

I'VE TOLD YOU WHAT IT IS TWICE NOW.

"YOU'RE A CITIZEN OF MEGA-CITY ONE..."

AND I'M SWORN TO PROTECT YOU.

I NEVER SAW JUDGE DREDD AGAIN.

OH, I *SAW* HIM, ON THE VID -- IN CHARGE OF JUDGES PUTTING DOWN A BLOCK WAR, OR SNARLING AT SOME TERRIFIED REPORTER -- BUT NOT FOR REAL, LIKE ON THAT MORNING WHEN I WATCHED HIM GO.

I GOT A LAST GLIMPSE AS THE LAWMASTER SPED BETWEEN A PAIR OF MOPADS, TAKING THE SUPER-FAST TO JUSTICE CENTRAL --

THEN HE WAS GONE IN THE ROAR AND CHAOS OF THE MEG...

AND AFTER THAT I NEVER HEARD FROM HIM AGAIN.

--DARIEN KENZIE

THE END

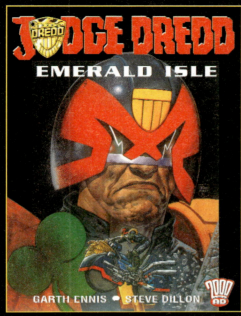
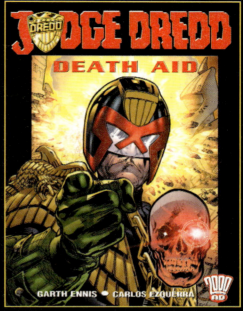
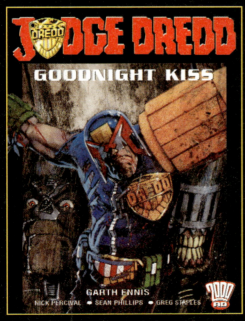